The Fox Wife

Published by Inhabit Media Inc.
www.inhabitmedia.com

Inhabit Media Inc. (Iqaluit) P.O. Box 11125, Iqaluit, Nunavut, X0A 1H0
(Toronto) 191 Eglinton Avenue East, Suite 310, Toronto, Ontario, M4P 1K1

Editors: Neil Christopher, Kathleen Keenan, and Grace Shaw
Art director: Danny Christopher
Designer: Sam Tse

This project was made possible in part by the Government of Canada.

We acknowledge the support of the Canada Council for the Arts for our publishing program.

Printed in Canada

Library and Archives Canada Cataloguing in Publication

Deer, Beatrice, author
      The fox wife / by Beatrice Deer ; illustrated by D.J. Herron.

ISBN 978-1-77227-212-3 (hardcover)

      1. Comics (Graphic works). I. Herron, D.J., 1994-, illustrator
II. Title.

PN6733.D433F69 2018   j741.5'971   C2018-905480-8

The Fox Wife

by Beatrice Deer

illustrated by D.J. Herron

One cloudless, starry night with no one in sight, a
fox fell from the sky and landed on its four legs on
a soft, mossy land.

She was a very pretty fox, with sharp, slanted dark
eyes and a coat of thick, flawless red fur.

The fox licked the fur of her paws straight and went on her way, exploring her new environment.

As she was walking along the hills, her sharp ears caught a new sound from a distance, a sound that was not the white bunting's chirping she had been hearing as she walked. Curiously and cautiously, she went toward the strange noise.

Before she saw where the noise was coming from, she caught a scent on the wind that she had never smelled before. She was even more intrigued.

Peering from behind a lichen-covered rock, she saw
a family, each member standing on their two feet,
setting up camp. They were humans—a woman with
her husband and two sons.

The woman was carrying her younger child in her *amauti*. The fox had never seen such a beautiful garment. The caribou-skin amauti was an ivory colour with silver edges of ringed-seal fur. The hood was lined with a beautiful dark fur. The fox was mesmerized.

LOOK, ANAANA, THE TENT IS ALMOST READY!

The fox watched as the family set up their camp. The man held up some long driftwood while his wife draped many sealskins sewn together over the wood to make a tent. The boy placed the large stones he had moved away earlier to hold the tent down along the bottom edges.

The fox couldn't take her eyes off the amauti. When she finally looked another way, her eyes immediately met the older boy's eyes, and she was startled. He had been quietly standing, watching the unaware fox.

The fox ran away. The next time she followed the family, she would be careful not to be seen.

Seasons came and went, and the fox continued to follow the family from a distance as they moved camp each season. The boy saw her from time to time, but the fox made sure not to get close. As she was a smart one, she learned the ways of the humans over time.

14

One day, it was time for the boy to leave his family and hunt on his own. He was now a young man.

Irniq set out on his own, with the fox following far behind.

The fox watched curiously as Irniq stopped to make a fire and boil water from the nearby lake in his small pot.

Irniq enjoyed the food and tea that had
been left for him. With a satisfied stomach,
he went to sleep.

The next day, Irniq woke up with a plan. He would pretend to go out on the land and hide behind a rock to see what happened around his camp.

After a while, he saw a fox enter his tent, and he slipped in after her with quiet steps.

23

YES, I AM YOUR WIFE, AND IT IS MY DUTY TO DO THESE THINGS. WHY, IS SOMETHING WRONG?

Not wanting to be alone, Irniq decided to accept her answer and keep her as his wife. Still, he wondered what had happened to the fox.

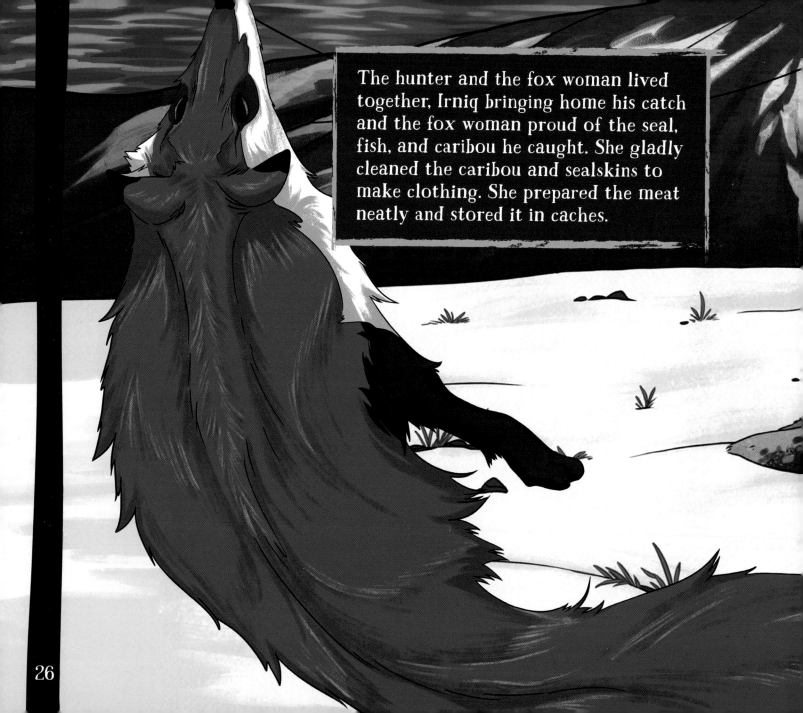

The hunter and the fox woman lived together, Irniq bringing home his catch and the fox woman proud of the seal, fish, and caribou he caught. She gladly cleaned the caribou and sealskins to make clothing. She prepared the meat neatly and stored it in caches.

26

After some time, the hunter noticed
something that the fox woman couldn't hide.
There was a musky smell about her.

Irniq persisted, and this made the fox woman
feel unwelcome.

But Irniq could not stop complaining.

Soon, Irniq went away hunting for several days. While he was gone, the fox woman decided she no longer wanted to stay where she was judged for the way she was, for she had no control over how she was created. She put her fox skin back on.

IF HE DOESN'T LIKE THE MUSKY SCENT I HAVE, THEN HE WILL NOT LIKE THE REAL ME.

And so she decided to walk away instead of being honest. She was too afraid to show him her real form.

The fox quietly slipped out onto the tundra. As she was about to go over the hill, she heard her husband calling and she turned around, looking back at the hunter, right into his eyes.

ARE YOU THE FOX I'VE SEEN FOLLOWING ME EVER SINCE I WAS JUST A BOY? **COME BACK!**

But the fox's mind was made up, and nothing could change it.
From her stare, in that moment, he understood.

She kept going, and she never returned.

Beatrice Deer is a singer, a seamstress, and an advocate for good health. Her skills as a seamstress were passed down to her from the women in her family in Quaqtaq, a tiny village on the most northeast coast of Quebec, in a region called Nunavik, meaning "massive land."

Beatrice has built up a group of musicians for her band—all talented in their own right—and they excel in allowing Beatrice's Inuktitut and English lyrics to soar over a pop folk-rock sound. Inuit culture and women's perspectives on life, love, and storytelling seep from all of Beatrice's music in an emotional and compelling way. Beatrice has four albums under her belt, including an award winner for Best Inuit Cultural Album at the 2005 Canadian Aboriginal Music Awards.

Beatrice has been based in Montreal since 2007. She travels north to perform and reconnect with her family on a regular basis. Connection to culture and a healthy lifestyle are all important aspects of Beatrice's life—her advocacy in this regard has made her a role model for many Inuit, young and old.

D.J. Herron is not a DJ Heron, a tall bird who spins sick jams. D.J. studied animation at Loyalist College, where she spent the bulk of her time designing characters, writing stories, and not being an avian mixmaster. When not storyboarding, sculpting, or designing monsters, she is likely to be found thumbing through fashion history and old medieval etiquette books.

Iqaluit • Toronto